MR. M[R]
on Hol[iday]
Roger Hargr[eaves]

Original conce[pt]
Roger Hargr[eaves]

Written and illust[rated]
Adam Hargr[eaves]

EGMONT

Little Miss Sunshine felt very sorry for Little Miss Scatterbrain when she heard about her holiday.

You see, last year Little Miss Scatterbrain went on a summer holiday.

But being the scatterbrained person she is she went to the North Pole!

It was a bit chilly for swimming.

Not really a summer holiday.

So this year, Little Miss Sunshine decided to organise Little Miss Scatterbrain's summer holiday for her.

And to make it really fun she invited along lots of Little Miss Scatterbrain's friends as well.

Everyone was very excited.

Mr Bounce jumped for joy at the news.

Which isn't such a good idea if you have as much bounce in you as Mr Bounce has!

Everyone set about packing.

Little Miss Sunshine packed all her things in her suitcase.

And then she went round to help Little Miss Scatterbrain who had packed all her things in her bookcase!

The next day everyone got the bus to the airport and boarded the plane.

And the plane took off.

Once Mr Greedy had moved seats, that is.

Mr Wrong decided to drive.

The first day of their holiday dawned bright and sunny and everybody headed to the beach.

In fact, they went to the beach every day that week.

And as each day passed, Little Miss Sunshine realised that she was going to have to help lots of her friends.

On the first day she had to show Little Miss Scatterbrain how to water-ski.

On the second day she had to show Mr Nonsense how to surf.

On the third day she helped Mr Topsy-Turvy.

He could not get the hang of eating ice cream.

Then Mr Silly went swimming in the sea.

Wearing his hat and shoes!

Little Miss Sunshine thought that was very odd.

Little Miss Scatterbrain thought it perfectly sensible.

The next day Little Miss Dotty made a sandcastle.

And Little Miss Sunshine made a sandcastle.

And Mr Muddle made an …

… ice-cream-castle!

Mr Greedy rather wished he had an ice-cream-castle.

On the last day they all played football on the beach.

Although it was the strangest game of football that Little Miss Sunshine had ever seen.

Little Miss Scatterbrain had a thoroughly wonderful week.

And Little Miss Sunshine felt thoroughly pleased.

It had all been a success.

Little Miss Scatterbrain brought back a souvenir.

Something to remember her holiday by.

She had packed it in her suitcase.

It was her …

… sandcastle!

What a scatterbrain she is.